THE
FIRST FLUTE

Whowhoahyahzo Tohkohya

DAVID BOUCHARD

the art of DON OELZE

the native flute of JAN MICHAEL LOOKING WOLF

Red Deer Press

Protocol

There are different versions of this story. This is the way it was told by Standing Elk, the late uncle of Jan Michael Looking Wolf. To honour Standing Elk and all his Relations, please adhere to the correct protocol of storytelling.

First, find a quiet place to share this telling. Do not allow for distractions. This telling is not long. You should be able to hear and dream it without disruptions.

Then, if you can, sit on Mother Earth, out in the open under Father Sky. If this is not possible, sit on the floor. Being close to Mother Earth is always good and it is particularly good when sharing a story.

And sit in a circle. Life's journey is a circle. We are born. We die. We grow taller. We become smaller. What goes up will come down. What we give away will always come back to us. A circle is best for sharing stories.

Now place both your hands on the earth or on the floor directly in front of you. Shut your eyes and listen for the sound of a distant Raven. Not everyone will be able to hear my voice but you might.

Listen to me. With your hands open on Mother Earth, you hear, feel and sense that there is nothing between us. Mother Earth gives us everything we need—water, food and shelter. All things are born of her. All things return to her. Crawlers, Flyers, Swimmers, Two- and Four-leggeds... we are all her children. We are all related.

The First Flute

Names are important.

Names should be respected. They should be valued. They should be honoured.

When a name is given to an adult, it is often given based on the life that person has lived. That name is a statement about the person he or she has become.

When a name is given to a child, it foretells what kind of a person that child will become. If a child is given the name He Who Is Kind to Strangers, that child is destined to live a life of kindness. I know this to be true because I once knew a kind man who as a child was given that name.

Chażeyatapi iyotan.
Chażeyatapi ahophe.
Chażeyatapi wankatuya.
Chażeyatapi yaonihan.

Tohan tuwa chażeyatapi kihan nina wopida nahoniyapi.
Tohan wichaśa chażeyatapi cha, hecha ewuthana mani kte.

Tohan chażeyatapi iyecheca mani kte. Tuwa chażeyatapi thoka ounśidapi. Tipi thipi Wichaśa chante waśte kihan thawachin waśte unkte.

Many winters past, there lived a young man who had been given the name Dancing Raven.

Dancing Raven lived on the plains—east of here—somewhere between the rising Sun and the dark, rolling hills.

There was nothing remarkable about where he lived... a shady village next to a rambling brook, foraging ponies, scattered smoking fires...

Ahuna wenayato hecktah wicasa wan Konhe Waci echeyapi.

Konhe Waci tintahtob ti,weyohinyohpahta, na we henapa heched na paha sapa heycheyta ti.

Hey eacha tipi wapa na hee, na sunkawakan wotape, hehun shota kaga.

However there was something special about Dancing Raven.

He was a dancer. He was the best and the most renowned dancer among all Nations.

He che Konhi Waci we cha, nina tohcha.

Waci wicasa heca, oyate ota nina waste keyapi.

From the day of his naming ceremony, Dancing Raven lived to dance.

As he and the other young men were taught to hunt and trap, Dancing Raven learned quickly, but he preferred dancing.

When he and the other young men were taught to race, shoot and wrestle, Dancing Raven excelled, but he preferred dancing.

Though he knew the prairies, mountains and the skies better than any other, Dancing Raven's heart was not in tracking. It was in dancing.

Heycha apato chazhayatahpi hehun Konhe Waci, waci wicasa heca.

Konhe Waci na kashapi wekanee weca hecape. E-ached ash waci cheen se.

Konhe Waci wekane weca na eyakapi na kote na kecezapi ospi keyapi. Konhe Waci nina waupeka.

Ma cochee ota stodya, tin da, paha na, mahpeyah gash Konhe Waci chonteh etuhun echushnee, wacis a ecena che.

Dancing Raven was wise and courageous and was often asked to lead the raiding party. Yet pride and success did not deter him from his desire to dance.

Konhe Waci nina k'sa-pah na tahkoon kokepa shnee. Hehon akeycheta too kaha cheenpe. Nina waste gash waci echana cheen.

Dancing Raven was often called upon to lead in
the Buffalo hunt. Yet his heart was in the dance.

Konhe Waci, ohena pte odaypi cheepe gash chonteh
etunhun waci echena cheen.

It was said that Dancing Raven was born with
a hand drum for a heart and the song of the
Meadow Lark as his Spirit Guardian.

Konhe Waci toon-pe hayhon chonteh chonchaygah hey
cha. Na odowan wa tahsheyahkah wa wakan ewankeypi.

As so often happens on one's journey through life, the young man Dancing Raven fell in love. When he had seen nineteen winters, he asked for the hand of the young woman of his dreams.

Tahun ne echa wana wicasa heyca Konhe Waci winyan tehida chee. Wana waniyetu week-chim-nah sum nopchin wonkah wana wonyahkah.

He asked, but her father, their Chief, refused.

"What can you offer my daughter?" the respected
Elder asked. *"What do you have to offer that has
any worth or value? Dancing will not feed my
daughter, nor will it feed my grandchildren."*

Wonyahkah nahey egadooza chee, wehumbia wonyahkah
gash winyan ate cheesnee, ate etuncha hecha.

*"Mecheenchena tako choo oyahkehey, gon ka ewoga. Tako
otageka oyakehe kte. Wacipi echena wota okehepkteshne
mecheenchena metakoosh."*

Struggling to conceal his tears, Dancing Raven made off for the comfort of the distant Sacred Hills.

These hills were said to be sacred because they were the home of the forest Elder, Grandfather Cedar. Though Grandfather Cedar had been ravaged by lightning and bore mostly bare and brittle branches, he stood tall and strong and was very much alive. Countless ceremonies had been held at his feet. Many important Chiefs had made their final journeys from that sacred ground.

Istamniyan heu cha Konhi Waci wakan paha heychea e.

Paha nina wakan keyapi. Onkan waziya ed tipi kayapi. Onkan hon teh sha wakinyah apape ash tahun wotana najin chonahdedkah edeapi gash wotuna najin. Wecokun ota se hata utapi na etuncha tona ed ehaka a he pe na hun maka wakan wagunkea ayapi.

As he laboured on his journey, the shattered youth stopped repeatedly to sing his prayer to Creator.

"Through song, dance and Tobacco, I give you thanks, Great Spirit. I ask only for your guidance. Please help me be strong. Show me the path to love. Help me, for I am weak and pitiful."

Tahun etoka manie, tona enajin na wakan dowaya.

Wakan Tanka na candi na dowan na waci. Omakey ya ho canku chont'kinyah maku, omkey ya, omasheka, na macooga.

His song was interrupted by a loud hammering that came from the hills. Sensing this might be the answer to his prayer, Dancing Raven raced toward the source of the sound.

Dear Reader, please understand that some sounds are born of one of the four Sacred Directions while others birth in Father Sky, Mother Earth or the fires that burn within each of us. The sound Dancing Raven heard came from the seventh direction—the Sacred Direction we have been taught to know as Love.

He soon found himself in the clearing that was Grandfather Cedar's home.

Dowan kte onkan taku paha haychea taku hotonka tonka kabooboo.

Dowan key hey wachekeya wakan nagunpe. Eyukchon, Konhe Waci duzonhon paha hechea e.

Heyche onkan b'dehzeh choka najin onkan nah hon teh sha tipi ed e.

There, high up on Grandfather Cedar, Woodpecker sat hammering on a hollow branch.

As Dancing Raven watched, the tapping stopped, a gentle breeze meandered into the hollow of the branch and from it came the most beautiful song he had ever heard.

As he listened, the heavy rolling clouds overhead darkened and a bolt of lightning shot down toward the majestic tree. The treetop shattered and the branch upon which Woodpecker had been perching came crashing to the Earth right at Dancing Raven's feet.

The insightful youth immediately recognized the gift for what it was. He reached into his pouch and withdrew a handful of Tobacco that he placed on the ground.

Dancing Raven quickly took his gift from Grandfather Cedar to a high ridge, raised it to his lips and imitated the song he had just heard... the song he had just been given.

Heyche onkan nah hontehsha tipi waguntuya chon kah doh dohnah chun ohchokah akun kabooboo.

Kohe Waci nagon najin onkan kabooboo enajin. Tate he onkan ohchokah hotoon onkan nina waste hotoon.

Nagoon najin onkan magpeya sapa hena onkan wahkinyah chun apae na kahk'sah.

Chun kahk'sah chonkahdohdohnah agun yakan hey, hinh'panyah Konhe Waci seha ed hinh'panyah.

Da tako toway magoo wo we yukchon nina waste makopi. Oh onkoh yah wozooha mahead candi echew na maka akun egdee.

Konhe Waci ohonkohyah whowhowahyahzo echew na paha hechea e na dowan wa ngun hey e-ached whowhowahyahzo oon e etonhun dowan hey whowhowahyahzo oon e-ached sh'kahtah, nina nagoo waste.

With that song in his heart, Dancing Raven
hurried back to the lodge of his love. He found
her there and played for her.

She listened, as did her father and the rest of
their village.

Dowan wa nagoon hey conta etonhon oon Kohe Waci
ohonkohyah winyan tageda hey tipi heychea e. Na winyan
eaya na whowhowahyahzo toon dowan sh'kahtah.

Wiyan dowan nagoon na, na ate egiaa nagoon. Nahun
oyate egeea nagoonpi.

Word of Grandfather Cedar's gift quickly spread across the plains.

Never before had a wedding attracted as many guests.

Never before had a couple received as many gifts.

Wakan Tanka hon tehsha wopeda whowhowahyahzo Konhe Waci koon na oyate tindak nagoonpi.

Winyan wah konkecheyuzahpe onkan oyate ota hepee.

Heyna takoon waste ota goopi.

And never before was a story shared by so
many across so many miles.

Tona hetoon kahkonpe oyate oyasay nagoonpi.

This book is dedicated to Makwa – for flutes,
friendship and so much more.

_____

Text copyright © 2015 David Bouchard
Illustrations copyright © 2015 Don Oelze
Music copyright © 2015 Jan Michael Looking Wolf

Published in Canada by Red Deer Press,
195 Allstate Parkway, Markham, Ontario L3R 4T8

Published in the United States by Red Deer Press,
311 Washington Street, Brighton, Massachusetts 02135

All inquiries should be addressed to Red Deer Press,
195 Allstate Parkway, Markham, Ontario L3R 4T8.
reddeerpress.com

10 9 8 7 6 5 4 3 2 1

Red Deer Press acknowledges with thanks the Canada Council for the Arts, and the Ontario Arts Council
for their support of our publishing program. We acknowledge the financial support of the
Government of Canada through the Canada Book Fund (CBF) for our publishing activities.

Canada Council   Conseil des arts
for the Arts   du Canada

ONTARIO ARTS COUNCIL
CONSEIL DES ARTS DE L'ONTARIO
an Ontario government agency
un organisme du gouvernement de l'Ontario

Library and Archives Canada Cataloguing in Publication
Bouchard, David
First Flute / David Bouchard ; illustrated by Don Oelze
ISBN 978-0-88995-475-5
Data available on file.

Publisher Cataloguing-in-Publication Data (U.S.)
Bouchard, David
First Flute / David Bouchard ; illustrated by Don Oelze
ISBN 978-0-88995-475-5
Data available on file.

Dakota translation: Wayne Goodwill
Cover and interior design by Tanya Montini
Printed in China by Sheck Wah Tong Printing Press Ltd.